The Boy Who Cried Wolf

CARAMEL TREE

Watching Sheep Is Boring

It is a warm sunny afternoon. Freddy sits under a tree. He watches the village sheep. The sheep walk and eat grass lazily around the field.

Taking care of sheep is boring. But it is Freddy's job. He must take care of the villagers' sheep.

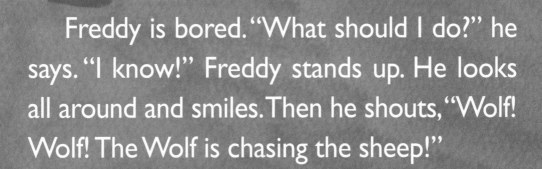

Freddy is bored. "What should I do?" he says. "I know!" Freddy stands up. He looks all around and smiles. Then he shouts, "Wolf! Wolf! The Wolf is chasing the sheep!"

The people from the village hear Freddy calling. They are worried for their sheep. They come running with sticks to help Freddy.

"Where is the Wolf?" they ask. The villagers look worried. Their faces are red. Freddy sees the villagers' worried faces and laughs.

"There is no Wolf." Freddy laughs again. The villagers are not happy.

"Do not cry Wolf when there is no Wolf," the villagers say.

Chapter 2

Freddy Lies Again

The next day is the same. Freddy takes the sheep to the field. He sits under a tree and watches the sheep eating grass.

Freddy is bored. He remembers his joke from the day before. Freddy smiles. Then he cries, "Wolf! Wolf! The Wolf is chasing the sheep!"

The villagers run to help Freddy. They bring sticks to chase the Wolf. But there is no Wolf.

Freddy laughs when he sees the villagers' worried red faces.

"There is no Wolf!" says Freddy.
"I was teasing you."
Freddy laughs again.
But the villagers are not laughing.
The villagers are angry.

The Villagers Don't Believe Freddy

On the third day, Freddy is watching the sheep. He feels bored again. He lies down and closes his eyes.

Suddenly, a big gray wolf jumps out of the bushes. The Wolf chases the sheep. The sheep run and cry, "Baah! Baah!"

Freddy sits up to look. Freddy sees the Wolf chasing the sheep. The sheep are trying to escape.

Freddy stands up and cries, "Wolf! Wolf! The Wolf is chasing the sheep!"

The villagers hear Freddy calling.
But they do not run to the hill.
"Oh, he is teasing us again," they say.

Freddy cries, "Wolf! Wolf! Please help me!" But nobody comes to help.

Freddy tries to save the sheep, but the Wolf is too big. Freddy cannot fight the Wolf alone.

Freddy is afraid. The Wolf chases all the sheep into the forest.

Too Late!

Freddy runs to the village.

"The Wolf chased and ate all the sheep," Freddy says.

Freddy starts to cry.

The villagers are confused. They follow Freddy to the field. All the sheep are gone.

"Why didn't you help me?" asks Freddy.

"Do not cry Wolf when there is no Wolf!" they say. "Nobody believes a liar even when he is telling the truth."

But it is too late now. The villagers have lost all their sheep.

Freddy sits under the tree and cries. "Next time, you must not tell a lie. Otherwise, no one will believe you," the villager says.

Freddy learns a lesson the hard way.
He will never lie again.